Teddy Roosevelt: Sasquatch Hunter

By Gayne C. Young

Teddy Roosevelt: Sasquatch Hunter

By Gayne C. Young

I greatly appreciate you taking the time to read my work. Please consider leaving a review wherever you bought the book or telling your friends about my book to help spread the word. Please visit me at my website www.gaynecyoung.com. While there, be sure to subscribe to receive free bonus chapters and photos, information on upcoming projects, news, and contest giveaways.

The bottle passed from hand to hand and around the fire, from John to Will to Karen and Louise then back to John again who pulled for a long turn, the flames reflecting off the glass and shimmering through the upended sea within. John lowered the bottle and exhaled the burn with a hearty laugh and he pulled Louise by her waist closer to him on the log they sat upon.

"Makes me feel alive," John declared to the group. He pulled his girl closer still and kissed her as she rejoiced in a playful attempt at shock. "The night air, whiskey, friends and my woman! Makes me feel alive."

"And the money from them furs you two got won't hurt that feeling none the less," Louise added.

"It's money from death." Will reached for the bottle and drank. "We're making a fortune off killing a bunch of small animals."

Louise sighed and Karen rolled her eyes at the comment.

"I' God if you ain't the killjoy there, Will," John mulled. "Take more after your mom, the Sunday School teacher than your father the reverend."

Will lowered his head and said, "Maybe so. Maybe so."

Karen took Will's shoulder into her hand and kneaded his hard muscle in attempt to quell the melancholy that lay at the surface.

"I meant to say we aim to do well off all them furs is all," Will explained. "We took us a lot of animals."

"That we did," John exclaimed.

Louise eased behind Will and went to work on both his shoulders and kissed his cheek then smiled at Karen.

"Karen, it's a good thing we brought the wagon to these boys. Month and a half out here has turned one sour and the other drunk on life."

"I am that!" John hooted. "I am that." He leaned into Louise and kissed her deeply and pulled back and took the bottle back from Will. He drank and stared at the full moon and then to its twin reflecting on the water below. Louise watched John in the moment and she ran her hand over his head and down his neck.

"Look at this wonder," John mused. "Right here in this crook of the Li'l Missouri River is paradise. Valley thick with forest and fur, space and beauty." John drank again. "I say we build us a cabin not far from where we sit and from here we can head further into the mountains for our money, down to the town for supplies, and live here in heaven in the middle."

Louise beamed from deep within and squeezed John tight around his broad chest. "Why, John are you about to ask what I think you're going to ask me?"

Will guffawed and Karen snorted with laughter at John's sudden look of unease.

John stammered, "Why I was just…"

Louise flipped John's hair in jest and kissed him for the stuttering fool he'd become.

"Did you see that look of sheer fright there, Karen?!" Louise laughed. "Sheer fright I tell you. The idea of a life from here on out done set him to nerves and stuttering."

John laughed at the place he found himself in then collected his composure and said, "That question might be coming soon enough. I know a place to get the metal. Just two days ago a group come down from them hills above. Prospectors. Said they made their year's wages in only ten days."

"A year's wage in ten days?" Karen bellowed in response. "Why I'd have stayed another ten days up there. Then another ten days after that."

"They were scared," Will mumbled. "That's why they came down."

"And there you go again, Mr. Down in the Dullards," John said. "They weren't scared of nothing."

"Yes, they were," Will corrected. "They were scared. Frightened. You could see it."

"Scared of what?" Louise asked.

"Scared of us or anyone else that saw the goods they was carrying would go up and take the rest of what they started, is what," John explained. "I never heard tell of a prospector yet that put out a shingle read, "I found the best place ever. The money litters the ground. Now let me tell you where it be so you can take it for yourself.""

Will reached for the bottle and took a long pull in an attempt to drown the feelings in his gut. Fear and doubt bloated in his lower extremities and the gas from the created cloud steamed upward and into the recesses of his soul. He was tired, spent after more than a month in the hills and beat from all that time running traps for mink and muskrat, weasel and beaver. The sight of carcass after carcass weighed on him and despite the money he and John stood to make from their efforts, Will began to see everyday in the hills as yet another in a long line of death. Just another day of killing. The sight of the prospectors' fears and the tale they told of their own encounter with death had twisted Will's last nerve. In a lot of ways John was right about his outlook on life. He was more like his mother than his father. Like she that bore him, he was prone to sadness and a feeder of misery when he encountered it.

John saw the depression in Will's face. He had seen it in his eyes and watched daily as they dimmed. John shot the bottle back toward Will and declared, "We're celebrating tonight my dear friend. Celebrating our haul and to our future, so drink up and drown them sorrows right."

Will took the bottle and drank.

Karen wrapped her legs and arms around Will from behind and squeezed. "I know a way to make my man feel good and proper," She boasted. "But it ain't a show meant for more than Will!"

Louise cackled and Karen blushed with sweet anticipation. John guffawed and reached out and slapped Will's knee. Louise stood and pulled John from the log. She eased into him and stood on tiptoes until she almost matched him face to face and said, "I've got a similar idea in mind for tonight but it'll require a bath fore it can commence for sure."

John kissed Louise and said, "I' God if ever I wished for a bar of soap."

Louise grabbed her bag from next to the log and bid John, "Follow me" and turned toward the river.

It was Karen's turn to cackle and she slapped Louise on the rump as she passed. John took the bottle from Will when he passed and joked, "If I'm not back in half an hour, don't come looking for me." Will promised he wouldn't and watched as the two walked toward the river.

Karen squeezed Will tight once more and he pulled her from behind him and into his lap. He took her face into his hands and pulled her lips to him. Karen eased back and placed her finger to Will's mouth and cooed, "Not just yet." She stood and offered, "This lady needs to visit the woods off yonder before I treat you right." Will nodded and watched Karen make a show of walking toward the darkness.

Louise stood at the water's edge wearing nothing but a smile, her pale skin the color of cream, a soft glow in the moonlight. She pulled the pins from her hair and John watched it cascade over her shoulders and down her back. She showed John the soap she held in one hand and with the other bid him trail her further into the river. John eagerly followed and when he came to her they embraced and they continued into the main channel as they held connected in kiss and tangled in the throws of passion. John broke and whispered, "This water's a might cold." Louise smiled and replied, "I can't tell that it's affected ya' none." John returned her smile and led them to the middle of the river where the water stood at chest level. Louise raised her chin and her long hair fanned out into the gentle current. She raised her head and gazed into John's eyes then dunked his head below the surface with a playful laugh.

The world aquatic engulfed him and the sounds from the atmosphere above stood muffled and echoed. Louise's giggling was a fair distance away and his ears focused instead on the beating of his heart, the current washing over him, and on his toes clicking the rocks beneath his feet. The moment was pierced by a faded cry and by the pull of Louise from in front of him. He shot upward to hear a woman's scream echo down the banks and to Louise's cry toward the fading fire. John turned his eyes toward the bank to see Karen's naked form running from the woods and to Will running toward her. The two met and from nowhere a shadow appeared between them. The darkness stood head and shoulders above Will's tall frame and with an explosion of movement it divided the couple from their embrace. Will flew backward through the air and into the fire. The flames exploded. Sparks shot outward and Will screamed with the pain of broken bone. His shirt flamed and he twisted and writhed in the coals in an attempt to free himself from the fire and to somehow make it back to Karen. Louise yelled toward the bank and rushed through the water toward shore. John yelled for her to stop but Louise steamed forward. John plowed toward her, yelling with each step for her to stop. Will rolled from the fire and tore the flaming shirt from his body. The air around him smelled of smoke and burnt skin and his eyes wept. He squinted through the pain and stood and rushed toward the hulking figure towering over the panicking Karen. He was met with the force of a tree falling against his chest and the last image he took from life was of the moon and the stars sailing above him. John hit the shore just as the looming figure pulled Karen from the ground by her neck. Louise yelled for her friend, to

God, and for mercy in a babbled nonsense of fear and a lack of control that she'd not felt since childhood.

John felt his leg slide out from under him on the slick rocks of the bank and he careened sideways and down. Adrenaline kept him from feeling the pain but his stomach turned at the sight of three inches of femur exiting his leg. He grabbed the protruding bone in primeval response and fought the urge to vomit. From that crippled position, he watched helplessly as the dark figure moved into the firelight to meet the determined Louise. He saw it as a man, taller and thicker in the chest than any he'd ever seen until he rationed that it must be a grizzly. Pain and the onset of shock turned in his head and he fought with what he witnessed.

Men aren't that huge; grizzles aren't shaped like that. The unidentifiable met Louise with the same force that it had met Will and her body twisted in the air as it flew backwards and into the edge of the fire. John sobbed watching as the thing returned to Karen and dragged her into the darkness. He lay there convulsing in pain and tears, questioning the events that had transpired, his actions, and his loss until the smell of searing flesh and singed hair drifted over him.

It was a smell he'd live the remainder of his life trying to forget.

2

"Theodore Roosevelt..."

Bill Marifield addressed the dozen men who stood in front of the bunkhouse. The spring air was crisp and the men actually attentive for once to hear what he had to say.

"...Is the new owner. From what I understand the deal was finalized back in January. He'll be here late this evening and although I have not heard one way or the other, I have no reason to believe that he plans on making any drastic changes. So for now, you all still have your jobs."

Some of the men sighed in relief while others stood in a trance of ignorance of such transactions or the feelings of not caring one way or the other. Jasper Carter stood before the others and only his face showed a look of genuine concern. He listened intently trying to study each of the ranch manager's words but his mind sped ahead to the questions he had and how he could turn things to his favor.

"If he does plan on any changes," Bill continued, " You all have my word that I'll fight for each and every one of you to keep your place."

Bill broke his gaze of a speaker before a crowd to give individual attention to the oldest of the group who leaned crutch in hand against the bunkhouse.

"Except you, Bauman," Bill smiled. "Doubt even the shiniest of silver tongued devils could sell the virtues of keeping a blacksmith with one bum leg on the ranch."

"I need only one leg to kick your sorry ass into the dirt little Billy Marifield," Bauman promised with a laugh. "And I' God if you'd be smart to remember that."

Bill smiled and the men chuckled at the exchange between men as comfortable as they.

"I don't like tell of a man," Bill returned to the group. "Rather let him and his actions speak for themselves. But Theodore is a good man…"

"When you meet him?" Jasper interrupted.

"He came to a property north of here to hunt bison last year. Wilmot Dow and I guided him. Theodore took a couple of nice bulls. He's a good fellow. Smart. Educated, but not enough to make him an ass."

"I never met an educated man that wasn't," Jasper countered.

"I doubt I'd tell him that to his face," Bill commented. "Might not help your long time employment none."

The men chuckled and Jasper felt the sting of shame pooling under the skin of his cheeks.

3.

Theodore's dream was twisted in vision, warped. His mind failed to focus on the images within, rather they rotated in vertigo like a child come off a merry-go-round. The voice was his, but distorted in volume and diction. He heard the words he had never spoken, only written, "The light has gone out of my life." He saw himself writing the words over and over again, "The light has gone out of my life. The light has gone out of my life." The journal on which they were scribed flipped backward in pages and the photos within came alive and he saw Alice, all of 19, fresh and ripe in courtship. Her features were fine and highlighted by youth. Her hair was raven black and her skin milk white and just as smooth as she carried him through almost four years of memories. Through engagement, the wedding, and the period of life after with all the joy that comes from living as a couple and learning to act as one. He saw his hand on her swollen belly, marveling at the life turning within. He felt once more the feeling of complete bliss knowing whatever the sex, the child would be nothing less than the best of her and him. A product of pure love.

But the vision morphed.

Colors faded and bled into a darkness of misery and sadness, fear and loss. He saw himself holding her in his arms as the clock above ticked louder and louder, each swing of the hand echoing, clap of thunder after clap of thunder. From further beyond came her voice soft and pure, soft and alive, soft and growing stronger. Her hand came from the darkness. He reached for her.

"Sir, sir."

Theodore shook. Fright pulled him into his seat. He reached for her. She took his hand in hers.

"Sir," she said. "I think you were dreaming."

Theodore jarred awake. He focused on the young girl looking at him then looked away in embarrassment. His eyes studied the landscape passing by his window and once adjusted, returned to the young lady. She smiled and looked to her hand within Theodore's. He pulled his from hers and let it fall to his lap.

"I said I think you were dreaming," she said once more.

"I'm afraid I was," Theodore stammered. His brow was heavy with sweat and his face flushed.

The young lady gave a smile of understanding.

"I hope I didn't bother you." He looked around the train car. Only she seemed to notice what he believed to be a spectacle on his part.

"Not at all," she eased. "I was just returning from freshening up to find you in distress. Not distress I should say, worried more like it. You looked bothered."

"That I was," Theodore said sitting straight in his seat. He adjusted his glasses back on the bridge of his nose. "Thank you for leading me from the darkness."

"Darkness?" she replied. "Sounds far worse than a dream."

Theodore saw and heard genuine concern. She was young but well mannered. Short with words but direct in meaning, not what he expected to find in North Dakota. He swallowed his feelings and assured the young lady that he was contented albeit embarrassed by his actions.

She assured him that there was no cause for such a thing and bid him a good rest of the trip and made her way down the train aisle to her seat only three rows behind him.

The next time he saw the young lady was on the platform of the station in Medora some two hours later. That meeting began when Bill met him with a firm handshake and a sincere "Welcome back." Bill smiled at

Theodore with genuine enthusiasm and then took the man's hand in his once more.

"Theodore," Bill's eyes locked on the man before him. "I am truly sorry for your loss. I cannot imagine…"

Theodore held Bill's hands tightly and raised the other hand to halt him.

"Thank you. I accept your condolences with an open heart knowing the type of man you are. Thank you."

Bill released his hand and smiled and slapped Theodore on the shoulder.

Theodore was lost in the moment and he looked to the horizon and to the ocean of blue above it. He smiled and searched for a response but instead returned with a story.

"When I was a child," Theodore began, "I was very weak. Deathly sick. I had asthma. Many an evening my mother would read to me well into the night, far past my bedtime, savoring our time together thinking it would be our last. Time passed yet my body didn't grow. My lungs stood shriveled, my muscles stagnant. The doctors told me that physical growth would come with rest. I disagreed. I decided to follow the example of those I admired in my reading. Boxers, warriors, soldiers, fighters. Hard work is what forged them and it's what grew me healthy. My plan is to work hard out here and with that work I shall…err…overcome…say, put to rest the hardship that has befallen me."

"Speak of the devil," Bill beamed. "Here comes my hardship."

Bill passed Theodore to embrace a young lady. Theodore recognized her from the train and immediately saw the look of family shared between she and Bill.

"Hardship?! I should hope not," she declared.

Bill hugged the girl tight then stepped from her to admire her. He held both her hands as if they were to dance then hugged her once more.

"Mr. Roosevelt," Bill began, "This is my daughter, Alexandra."

The young lady turned to Theodore and smiled in recognition.

"We've already met," she declared. "Although we've not been properly introduced."

Theodore tipped his hat and declared, "It is a pleasure to meet you Miss Alexandra."

"Alex will do fine," she countered. "I meant to say I prefer Alex to Alexandra, it's much less formal."

"That it certainly is," Bill offered in the way of a father partially questioning social decorum.

Alex returned with a look of daughterly comeuppance then continued her introduction. "I so wish I had known who you were on the train. I could have fielded your questions about the ranch – if you had any that is. I've lived there my entire life and dare say I know it like the back of my hand."

Bill sported a slight frown and nodded.

"Knew it until I was shipped away to learn the ways of the eastern seaboard lady-hood, I should say."

"And a good place for you," Bill chided.

"Your thoughts on a woman's place, Mr. Roosevelt?" Alex asked with raised eyebrow.

"Don't bring Theodore into this…" Bill instructed.

Theodore laughed, "I'm not sure that I came all this way to get in an argument between father and a daughter."

"Completely understandable," Alex said.

"But that being said," Theodore interrupted. "My senior thesis back in 1880, my that was four years ago now, was titled *The Practicality of Equalizing Men and Women Before the Law.* I argued quite well that men and women should be equal and women should be able to make up their own…"

Bill dropped his head in mock distress. "I can't wait to introduce you to the boys back at the ranch. They'll get a kick out of you and your comments like that for sure."

Alex waited on baited breath for Theodore and when he burst into laughter she followed.

"I bet they will," Theodore blustered. "Yes, I expect they will."

4.

Two Nights dismounted his horse and led it by the reins slowly over the upended sod and turned dirt toward the fallen cow. The earth around the heifer painted a mosaic of past struggle and violence. An eighteen-inch furrow showed where the Hereford's horn plowed through the ground and into death. Veins of dried snot spider webbed outward from the body and coagulated blood pooled beneath the animal's nostrils. The beast's eyes were hemorrhaged and the placement of its head in relation to its body told that it died from a broken neck. Two Nights' horse snorted at the scene of death and did all that it could to retreat from the body that lie contorted in death. Two Nights comforted his horse and led it to a stand of hardwood some twenty yards away and tied it to a limb. He returned to the fallen cow and continued his study.

The animal had been partially eaten along the hook-bone where huge chunks of muscle had been ripped from along the spine. Two Nights ran his fingers over the sun-dried flesh looking for the telltale signs of claw marks or the puncture wounds of heavy canine teeth but found none. He backtracked the path that led to the animal's fall and upon the torn ground looking for spoor and found only the rounded imprints of something he couldn't identify. He thought for a time that they were left by a grizzly but the deep rounded tracks showed no signs of claws. This, combined with the fact that grizzlies don't run on two feet, led his thoughts elsewhere. He left the scene believing that the cow had been killed by a grizzly and that for the majority of the attack the bear had been embedded upon the animal's back haunches. Several times the grizzly's rear legs had hit the ground with only the pads of its feet but it had lunged forward and back on top of the cow almost immediately in an effort to drop the animal.

At least that's what Two Nights told himself.

5

Theodore arrived at breakfast dressed every inch the manner in which he expected a cowboy would dress. He stood before Alex and Bill covered head to toe in buckskin, and sporting heavy boots, a hat, and a bandana. His belt held twin Colt .45 revolvers, a Bowie knife, and a coiled bullwhip.

"I do believe I am ready to face the day," he joyously declared.

Alex smiled over her coffee and Bill dropped his chin to hide his smiling disbelief.

"And a hell of a day it would have to be to go dressed like that," Bill offered.

Alex play-slapped her father's hand and covered her smile.

"I think you are the very picture of a cowboy adventurer, Mr. Roosevelt," Alex explained.

Theodore sat and allowed Alex to pour his coffee. "If I am to call you Alex then you are to call me Theodore."

"That fall in line with your view on men's and women's equality?" Bill jokingly questioned.

"Theodore," Alex pondered aloud. "If you don't mind my suggestion, I should think T.R. sounds more of the rugged cowboy than does Theodore."

Theodore lowered his coffee and exclaimed, "T.R.! I like the sound of that. T.R. the cowboy is fine. Truth be told, anything other than Teddy is fine with me."

"Then T.R. it is," Alex declared.

"Now that we've settled how we will be referring to one another," Bill began. "Might we go over the day's agenda?"

Alex giggled and sat her head upon her folded hands resting on the table and batted her eyes towards her father. "Shall we?"

Bill shook his head and waved his daughter onward with his napkin, "Go in the kitchen and see what's keeping Gladys with breakfast."

Alex made a show and left T.R. and Bill to the matters of the day before them.

"I know you originally wanted a tour of the facilities and to meet the men," Bill recalled. "But I might have something more interesting."

"I'm game for anything. Especially anything strenuous taking place out of doors in this clean, clean air," T.R. confessed.

"This would involve that," Bill hinted. "How would you feel about a grizzly hunt?"

"A grizzly!" T.R. nearly launched from his chair. *"Ursus arctos horribilis.* Hunting one of these magnificent beasts would be bully!"

"I knew you'd be excited."

"More than words can convey."

Bill explained that his top ranch hand Two Nights had come across evidence of a grizzly kill just the day before and that once a bear gets a taste for beef there's no turning him away from it. The marauding bear would have to be killed. T.R. agreed and when breakfast was brought he wolfed it down with the fervor of a child ripping into presents on Christmas morning in anticipation of heading afield.

All the ranch hands were ready and assembled when Bill led T.R. into the yard.

T.R. looked the men over and announced, "I look forward to meeting each and every one of you but I'm afraid I'm unable to do so at this time for I'm off to hunt a grizzly."

The men stood dumbfounded by the man before them. None had seen a man so giddy nor heard a voice that raced so fast on each breath of air. Then there was the matter of T.R.'s clothes and weaponry that seemed only to punctuate the oddity that stood before them. To Jasper though, T.R. was more than odd. He was a foreigner. He was someone who didn't belong.

"Now," T.R. changed course, "Which one of you is Two Nights?"

The men looked to each other in confusion, unsure if T.R. was joking or not. Bauman shook his head and laughed then slapped Two Nights on the back and forward from the group.

"This is him. Only Indian in the bunch."

T.R. watched as the man came from the group. The man stood taller than the rest and his skin and hair were far darker than those around him as well. T.R. burst into laughter, "Ha, I suppose I could have made that assumption now couldn't I have?"

Unsure of anything concerning the new owner, the men joined T.R. in heavy laughter.

6.

The newness of T.R.'s saddle creaked with each step of his mount. At first Two Nights ignored the give and take of the freshly tooled leather riding next to him but after a half hour he could stand it no longer.

"I've never seen a saddle quite that…," Two Nights paused in thought, searching his mind for the right word.

T. R. beat him to the punch and offered to finish the sentence left undone.

"Nice?"

"Uh, no."

"Ornate?"

"No."

"Cumbersome?"

"Does that mean too big for what it is?"

T.R. laughed and said that it more or less did.

"Yes, then, it is cumbersome."

"Well I can't say that the man who crafted it had ever made a western saddle before. Makes many fine English saddles though."

"He did a good job on the scabbard," Two Nights said, glancing at the dark oiled leather.

"Thank you. I think so as well. I had him craft it around the rifle specifically." T.R. pulled the rifle from its holster and handed it to Two Nights. Two Nights checked the gun and held it tight to his shoulder then passed it back to T.R.

"It's a Winchester .45-75. Shorter version of the .45-70," T.R. declared. "That a good caliber for grizzly?"

Two Nights replied in stoic tone, "Bear will let you know real quick if it's not."

T.R. looked for reassurance at Two Nights' statement then burst into deep laughter at the Indian's telling smile.

"Bully!" T.R. expelled. "Absolutely bully!"

The two men continued their steady pace across fields of spring grasses towards a distant mesa. T.R. marveled at the rich yellows and lavenders of the few flowers that dotted the sea of green grass before him. He looked in awe at the cyan blue of the sky above and with geological interest at the rows of browns that composed the distant hills. He relished in the sounds as well, the breathing of the mounts, the whine of the insects, the calls of birds in the distance, and the give and take of his new saddle beneath him. He suddenly became conscious of the latter and decided conversation was the best way to muffle the sound.

"Are your people from this area?" T.R. asked.

"You mean the other ranch hands?" Two Nights again returned to a look of stoicism but was unable to keep it in the face of T.R.'s questioning glance of *faux pas*. The two men laughed at T.R.'s embarrassment before Two Nights returned to the question at hand. "Yes. My people are from this land. I am Salish."

"But your head isn't flattened," T.R. observed.

Two Nights pulled tight on the reins in his hands bringing his mount halt. "How do you know about that custom?" he asked in shock.

T.R. halted his horse and adjusted his glasses. "I meant no offense…"

"I am not offended. Just…curious."

"I read about the flatheads in the diaries of Lewis and Clark. I'm a voracious reader. Especially on matters of the wild. Of the frontier."

Two Nights eased his horse forward and T.R. followed.

"My mother was a Christian. Converted by a Black Robe. Pierre-Jean De Smet."

"I've read his words on your people as well…"

"He taught my mother the ways of Christ and that modifying her son's head wasn't Godly," Two Nights explained. "I can't say that I missed having it done to me."

"I imagine so. Interesting body modification though." T.R. pulled his horse tight to watch a tortoise lumber next to the trail then kicked his horse sharply to catch up to Two Nights. "Say your mother was Christian. Yet your name…"

"Two Nights? It is more Christian that what I was to be called."

"And that was?"

"It took my mother two nights to deliver me and when I finally came she announced, "Thank Christ The Little Bastard Is Finally Out Of Me." Father De Smet said that although that was most certainly a fitting name it wasn't very socially acceptable."

T.R. doubled over in laughter at the story and stayed that way for some time.

The men rode higher into the hills on trails of earth flattened by cattle and through fields of scrub brush teeming with songbirds and the heavy buzzing of insects. They skirted a stand of hard woods and rode onto a butte where the fallen cow lie bloated with gases and teeming with clouds of flies. Both mounts became uncomfortable at the smell of death and Two Nights led T.R. to the place where he had tied his horse the day prior.

"Grizzly did this?" T.R. asked as the men walked to the dead animal.

"More or less," Two Nights answered in avoidance. "That's what took her down anyway. The rest of this was coyote, buzzards."

T.R. looked to the canine tracks before the animal's opened gut and asked, "Coyote?"

Two Nights nodded and moved up wind.

For all his life, everything had been an opportunity to learn for T.R. He questioned Two Nights about the animal tracks around the cow, about the torn earth, and how long it would take for nature to fully reclaim the animal. He asked about the breed's resilience in the harsh Dakota winter, the distance it moved each day, and the grasses that it preferred. And when he was done questioning about the cow he turned to its killer.

"Why would a grizzly take down a cow?" He asked. "Do bears prefer this over say deer or is it a matter of ease of kill?"

Two Nights explained that all wild animals were the same. They wanted to live, breed, and eat and they looked to the easiest path to do each of these. A bear won't exert extra energy for one animal over another. He'll kill and eat what is the easiest to do so and when options are limited, it will take what is available.

"Years ago," Two Nights began. "This land held buffalo, deer, and big horn. Today it holds cows. A grizzly will eat what is available."

"Much like people," T.R. pondered.

"Exactly like people," Two Nights replied.

7

Jasper watched Alex from afar. He studied her movements as she arranged the flowers she gathered from the fields in a small vase on the table on the porch of the main house. She had matured greatly in the year that she had been gone. She exhibited no holdover from girlhood. She was fully a woman and a beautiful one at that. Although Jasper remembered little of her mother he figured Alex followed her closely. She stood tall for the period and carried more strength in her features than she did femininity. She was beautiful and strong, womanly yet tough. Jasper waited until her back was turned to approach. He called to her just short of the steps to the porch. She turned and smiled fully at the joy of seeing an old friend.

"Jasper!" She exclaimed.

"Hello, Alex."

The two hugged then separated to apprise one another in different ways and for different reasons.

"I was wondering when I'd see you," she admitted before gesturing for the young ranch hand to sit. The two sat in rattan chairs set next to one other on the porch. "How have you been?"

"I've been well," Jasper offered. "Your father is keeping us busy."

"Of that I am sure." Alex chided. "He is never one to let a moment pass without some production."

Jasper smiled and nodded then asked, "How's your school been going?"

"It is what it is." Alex semi-moaned. "I love my classes, I really do, but could do without all the politics and formalities involved."

Jasper held his smile, watching Alex speak and watching the way in which she did so.

"But who wants to hear about all that?" Alex asked.

"I do," Jasper readily admitted.

"No, that life must seem like such a bore to you. Tell me about your doings. I thought maybe you'd be off starting your own place by now, married and on your way to building a huge family."

"I've always wanted that," Jasper confessed. The joy in his eyes changed to seriousness. "But who I wanted to do that with – always planned to do that with – hasn't been around."

Alex saw and felt the change in Jasper. She saw now a man looking to change his life rather than the boy she had grown up with.

She had seen that look in men back East and it left her feeling ill at ease and completely vulnerable. It was a feeling she didn't quite understand and one she had yet to come to terms with.

"Have you met the new owner yet?" Alex changed directions.

Jasper stammered that he had but briefly.

"He's the most wonderful man," Alex assured him. "He reminds me a great deal of father. Dry sense of humor. Very bright, although with new and liberal ideas."

Jasper scowled.

8

Two Nights led T.R. through the hills and into a valley below where they made camp on the banks of the Little Missouri River. Two Nights said that from there they would glass the hills for grizzly in the early dawn. But the truth was he liked the area and he liked camping there. They made a fire and cooked steak and potatoes then stoked the fire and sat in its glow to enjoy the remainder of the night.

"Seeing that cow today," T.R. began, "Reminded me of the first animal I ever dissected. It was a seal. Some fishermen had it on the docks."

"An eel?" Two Nights questioned. "They look like a snake, do they not?"

"No, a seal."

"What is a seal?"

T.R. thought for a moment then offered. "It's an aquatic mammal; similar to a whale, I suppose. Only smaller."

"The fish that swallowed Jonah in the Bible, " Two Nights related.

"Exactly, only a seal is much smaller, about seven feet I suppose and has flippers instead of a tail."

Two Nights mulled this over and nodded in the radiant light.

"I was just a boy," T.R. continued. "I took it home and dissected it much to the chagrin of my parents, my mother especially."

"What did it taste like? Did it taste like whale?"

"I've not eaten either so I can't say."

"What did you learn from dissecting this seal?"

"That I'm not very good at dissecting seal."

T.R. laughed at his own admission and Two Nights chuckled in response and threw another log on the fire before asking, "What is it like to be so learned?"

"I wouldn't say that I'm so…"

"Mr. Merrifield said that you went to Harvard and that you wrote a book on Naval Warfare."

"I did, but…"

"And you told me just now about dissecting an animal to learn about it."

"I've had a great many opportunities," T.R. modestly admitted. "And it's true I always desire to learn more but I'll tell you something about intelligence my father told me. He told me that the more you learn the more you learn how much you don't know."

"Your father too was wise," Two Nights complimented.

"He also told me that the smartest thing a man can do is to admit to not knowing something."

Two Nights nodded in agreement and let his mind wander. He thought of what he had learned in life and the two very different cultures he had learned from. He pondered the things he knew and then wondered how many things he knew that weren't worth knowing. He then focused on what T.R. had just related, "The smartest thing a man can do is to admit to not knowing something."

Two Nights stared across the fire at T.R. and admitted, "That cow was not killed by a grizzly. I don't know what killed it."

T.R. sat forward in both disbelief and heavy anticipation.

"What do you mean?"

"There are grizzly here but a bear didn't kill that cow. I do not know what did. It carried tracks unlike any I'd seen before. Whatever it was though, it was very large and very strong. It killed the cow by snapping its neck."

"And a grizzly couldn't do that?" T.R. sounded almost disappointed.

"I don't believe so."

T.R. approached the situation as he did with most unknowns in his life – through questions and study.

"The only spoor of the animal was its tracks?"

"Yes."

"Tell me about them."

"They were very large. Like a man's but much bigger and with the toes spread much more so. It walked on two legs and sometimes four."

"Were both sets of prints the same?"

"No, the front tracks looked like a man's fist had punched the ground."

"What you're describing sounds like a gorilla."

"What is a gorilla?"

"An ape, a close relative of man. It's a large hairy beast that walks on two legs as well as on its knuckles." T.R. leaned over to demonstrate the stance he'd described. He righted himself and continued, "They were only recently discovered in Africa. I saw some taxidermy mounts that a hunter by the name of Paul du Chaillu brought to New York."

"And it looked like a hairy man?"

"A man in figure yes, only much larger and far stronger."

Two Nights processed what was being said then tilted his head in thought and said, "This gorilla sounds like Sésquac, a wild man from Salish lore."

"Gorillas were considered lore, a myth for generation until Mr. Du Chaillu bagged one."

"So you were saying there could be a gorilla here?"

"I'm saying, show me the tracks tomorrow."

9

Centuries of selective breeding has failed to completely remove all of the wild from domestic animals. Dogs still desire to kill as did their wolf ancestors, cats long to be solitary, and cattle still inherently herd for protection. And such was the case with the five Herefords that stood guard with one another under the ghostly pale moonlight. The lead female stood taller than the rest and closer to the tree line although not by much. Even in sleep she was alert. The ancestral part of her brain processed every sound and every smell for danger.

It was the latter that woke her.

A sudden yet faint scent in the air warned of a predator. She could smell the hunger of the animal approaching and the high testosterone and adrenaline flowing throughout it and driving it forward. The matriarch vocalized the danger and the herd responded with grunts and bellows. The youngest and smallest of the herd broke in retreat and in doing so became the easiest target.

The predator exploded from the tree line on two legs then fell to four in a sort of semi-sideways gallop. It lunged forward and through the air coming to land beside the fleeing Hereford. It grabbed the bovine's horns in massive hands and wheeled them until the sound of vertebra shattering clapped like thunder through the night. The cow dropped on a small grouping of rock and its neck opened on jagged shards. A fountain of warm blood slopped from the jugular and pooled over the rock and onto the prairie.

The predator stood and beat its chest in triumph and roared its dominance through the still night air. It dropped to the side of its kill and lifted the head and dropped it again if only to assure that it was truly dead. Satisfied, it opened the wound with pry bar fingers and ripped flesh from bone and gorged.

10

T.R. was dancing with Alice once again.

The two young lovers spun in perfect unison around the dance floor before a crowd of guests intoxicated by their beauty and at the celebration of their hour's old nuptials. T.R. loved the feel of the small of her back beneath his hand and her hand upon his shoulder. She smelled of powder and spring flowers and appeared at that moment more beautiful than ever before. She was the love of his life and would be forever.

A slow tide of darkness washed over the room. Guests ceased to exist and tables and chairs disappeared in the ever growing void of light. T. R. was no longer holding his love, rather he watched from some ether as one by one and object by object the room vanished. The tunnel closed on Alice's face and T.R.'s words echoed in her voice, "The light has gone out of my life."

Then nothing, only darkness and an infinite expanse of midnight black remained.

There was no past.

There was no present.

There was no future.

The void was broken by a scream so fierce, so primeval that it could only come from the bowels of hell. T.R. thrust upward and awake. He couldn't catch his breath. He was soaked in sweat and shivering in the night air.

Two Nights came from his bedroll, a Bowie knife the length and girth of a child's arm gripped his hand. He looked across the half lit coals to T.R.

"It's nothing…" T.R. stammered in embarrassment. "Nothing. I heard a scream."

Two Nights sheathed his knife and raised the fire with tender.

"A scream?"

"More of a roar like a bear. Blood curdling. You didn't hear it?"

"I heard you," Two Nights answered.

"It wasn't me.." T.R. assured him. "I was dreaming, yes, but I was awakened by a …by that roar."

Two Nights nodded in appeasement.

"I swear I heard it." T.R. continued, "I did. I heard it."

In a small opening nestled between two stands of trees, up river from where T.R. and Two Nights were camped, the origin of the scream ripped another handful of flesh from its kill and fed.

11

T.R. was unable to return to sleep for the remainder of the night. At first he lie watching the flames of the rebuilt fire twist and snake in consuming adulation before fading to red coals. He studied the moon above him and ran through the constellations and the mythology behind them and their coming to be. Sure that he wouldn't find slumber again, he fed the fire until it was light enough to read. He read until his pocket watch said it was close to dawn and he made coffee and watched as the sun burst blood red over the buttes across the river. He was watching several does drink in the shallows when Two Nights rose.

"Have you spotted a grizzly yet?" Two Nights asked as he reached for the coffee.

"I thought you said what killed that cow wasn't a grizzly," T.R. verified.

"I did." Two Nights paused to drink, burned his lips, blew on his coffee and tried again. "But that doesn't mean we won't see a grizzly and if we do, you should shoot."

T.R. agreed, "I've been thinking…"

"You do that a lot," Two Nights cajoled.

"How very true." T.R. laughed and said. "Your grizzly comment brings me to a thought I had earlier. Grizzlies are omnivorous. They eat both plants and animals."

Two Nights agreed.

"How much will a grizzly weigh out here?"

"Merrifield shot a boar two years back that went almost 600 pounds."

"Right then. The gorillas that Du Chaillu took in Africa averaged around 300 to 350 pounds for males. The females averaged around 200…"

Two Nights grinned at following T.R.'s thought process. "You're thinking of food."

"Precisely. If this area can support a 600-pound omnivore then it can certainly support a 350 pound one. Of course that's just part of the equation but it certainly merits further study."

"And that further study?"

"Again, I think identifying the tracks is a good idea."

"We can do that." Two Nights killed his coffee. "They'll be difficult to read following everything that has come to feed on the cow."

"I have complete faith in you."

T.R. and Two Nights broke camp and mounted their horses after allowing them to drink their fill at the river. They ate hardtack as they rode up river and filled their canteens then skirted a butte and made their way into the hills. They rode through short prairie and through stands of cedar and juniper heavy with fruit and clouded with pollen and bees. They were witness to a golden eagle take a prairie dog and saw a rafter of eight turkeys flee from before their path into some scrub. By mid-morning they were half way to the fallen cow when Two Nights pointed to a cyclone of vultures and crows circling the sky to their east. Two Nights said that if he were riding alone he'd be required to investigate the cause of such a gathering of scavengers. T.R. responded that nothing should be different on his account. They turned their mounts and headed east towards the quarter arched sun. It wasn't long before the smell of rot and decay was on them. Shortly after that Two Nights spotted its source on a small rise only 200 yards before them.

Two Nights shook his head in disgust. "Another cow."

T.R. dug his heels into his mount and galloped for the dead heifer. At fifty yards from the carcass T.R.'s horse fought its commands and shook its head and wrestled to a stop. T.R. kicked his heels into the horse's sides and the horse reluctantly moved forward. At twenty yards to the rise where the cow lay the mount whinnied nervously and bucked in fear. T.R. pulled tight on the reins but was thrown clear and he came to land on his back with such a hard blow that the wind was knocked from him. He stood and immediately felt light headed. He watched in a daze as his horse sped away. He heard Two Nights yell something and saw him thrust his arm in point. T.R. turned to see the cow's belly hide rise then explode in a movement of violence and speed he had never witnessed before. Seven foot of grizzly roared forth; its muzzle dripping with blood, its teeth flashing yellow decay. The bear dropped to four legs and shot forward and over the cow. T.R. pulled his Colt and fanned the hammer. Lightning flashed from the muzzle in quick succession and each blast clapped in thunder. The bear lunged forward and stood on hind legs. The click of the empty cylinder roared louder than the shots prior. T.R. braced himself as 500 pounds of predator fell on top of him. The world went dark and he could barely breath. He could feel the damp warmth of the bear's muzzle against his head and he struggled desperately to free himself. He was reaching for the Bowie on his belt when he heard a muffled call but the crushing weight upon him kept him from calling in return. He felt the last strength of his ribs giving way to the force exerted on them when there was a tinge of relief. Then he saw sun.

"T.R.!" Two Nights yelled as he rolled the bear. "Push! Push him!"

T.R. did and with this added help they were able to roll the boar over and off of T.R. Two Nights let forth a stream of words so guttural and with such force that T.R. knew them to be Salish profanity.

Two Nights slipped back into English, "Holy, holy, holy shit!"

He pulled T.R. from the ground. T.R. stood on wobbled legs then ran his hands over his person searching for broken bones. There were none but his glasses were wish boned against his face albeit not broken.

"You alright?" Two Nights blared. "Take a minute. You ok?"

Before T.R. could answer Two Nights burst into hysterical laughter.

"Holy shit!" he exclaimed. "You got him twice between the eyes!"

T.R. saw the two holes almost touching between the bear's eyes.

"Where...where? I shot six times...Where?"

"You fired six Hail Marys and two took."

"I am not a good shot but I shoot often."

"Good thing!" Two Nights exclaimed slapping T.R. on the back. "Hell'uva good thing."

Emotions raced through T.R.

Fear, joy, and exhilaration pulsed through his veins and pooled in his heart. He thought he'd explode.

And he did.

"Bully!"

12

The ranch hands cheered T.R. as a hero when he rode up with seven foot of grizzly strapped to the back of his horse and cheered even louder still when Two Nights told briefly of the great beast being slain with two shots at close range. The cook examined the bear and instructed that a large fire be built. Bill came to look at the bear and told the men to make the fire even larger than planned as there'd be a celebration that evening. Alex congratulated T.R. with a hug and a kiss to the cheek and made him promise to tell her all about the hunt after she helped make preparations for the impromptu feast. Jasper saw the kiss and fumed. He returned to the bunkhouse and removed a bottle he had stored in his kit and took a heavy pull.

And then another.

Bauman crutched over to see the bear and joshed Two Nights to admit he'd shot the bear and not this Easterner wearing glasses pressed into his face. Two Nights laughed as did T.R. and Two Nights promised that he had seen the whole thing transpire and that T.R. was as fast on his feet as they come. T.R. cajoled that he was as fast as could be when scared to death of being eaten by a bear. Bauman called one of the feet and licked his lips exclaiming that he hadn't had mud-packed bear feet straight from the coals since Merrifield took his bear two years prior. Bill said that eating one of the bear's best cuts of meat would be at the discretion of the grizzly killer at hand.

"But," Bill addressed T.R. "Might I suggest that you save two feet for Sylvane and Ferris as they'll be riding out shortly."

The two ranch hands voiced their complaints and Bill said that their objections were duly noted but they'd still be riding out to check cattle anyway.

"That grizzly's killed two cows already and probably scattered the herd three valleys over. I want you two to round up any that did and bring them closer in."

Sylvane and Ferris accepted their assignment and asked T.R. to save them two feet.

T.R. replied, "I'd be glad to. Thank you gentlemen for your service."

The two hands left joking that they'd never been addressed as gentlemen in all their lives. Jasper returned to the scene with four good shots of whiskey in him. He approached just in time to hear T.R. ask Bill if Alex would care for the other foot.

Jasper blurted, "Is that how you impress girls back in New York? Give them a bear foot cooked in a ball of sod?"

Bill shot Jasper a look of warning.

T.R. chuckled and replied, "I doubt the offer would win the heart of any a New York lady."

"So Alex is beneath them?" Jasper taunted.

"Jasper," Bill boiled. "Go help with the fire. Now. "

Two Nights pulled T.R. to the now off loaded bear.

"Look at his foot," Two Nights said holding up the bear's front right paw. The bear's extremity was bent downward and its claws curved underneath like sharp sickles.

"What is this?" T.R. asked.

"I'd guess he broke his paw and it healed wrong. The claw's bent wrong like that and he couldn't wear them down. They just continued to grow."

"Track you saw?" T.R. said.

Two Nights rolled the dead appendage in his hands. "It has to be."

T.R. sighed in slight disappointment.

"Makes more sense than a gorilla," Two Nights said uneasily.

"I enjoyed our speculation on the matter regardless," T.R. said.

Two Nights said he had as well and helped two ranch hands and the cook move the bear to be processed.

"Overheard you say something about a gorilla," Bauman inquired to T.R.

T.R. turned to address the man and said, "Yes, it's rather silly."

"A joke? I love a good one."

"No. No it wasn't a joke. Do you know what a gorilla is?"

"Sure, seen pictures in the paper of those touring big cities back East."

"Well, Two Nights found some tracks that resembled those of a gorilla. He described them as a man who had punched the earth. Knuckle prints would be a better description I suppose."

"Where?" Bauman's question came quick and sharp. He seemed suddenly flustered.

"The hills above the bend in the Little Missouri River."

Bauman's face drew gray. Beads of sweat appeared on his brow. His body slumped against his crutch.

"Turned out it was simply the grizzly's deformed paw," T.R. explained.

"Let's hope so," Bauman muttered on forced breath. "Let's hope to God."

The fire burned high as the sun began its descent. A table was brought out of the main house as were chairs and buffets. One of the ranch hands brought out his fiddle and the air was filled with music. T.R. watched with great interest as the cook seasoned each of the bear's feet with a heavy powdering of cayenne, salt, and black pepper and packed them each in balls of wet mud and buried them in the coals. The bear's body proper was placed on a spit above the coals and the smell of grease dripping into the fire sent all the men to salivating. Bill allowed the drinking of spirits if the men promised to control themselves. He then took Jasper aside and in gruff voice said, "I don't know what set you off and truth be told I don't give two rats' asses to hear about it but you listen to this - straighten up or you'll be out of work faster than your half-way pickled brain can process it."

Jasper nodded and apologized and stood away from the men sulking his reprimand and at the men's enjoyment. He'd almost put the matter out of his head until he saw Alex make her way through the fire to T.R. Anger and jealousy boiled in him as he watched her hand T.R. a glass of wine and how he grinned from ear to ear as he took it from her.

T.R. thanked Alex for the wine and toasted her glass. "Here's to a successful hunt," he said as the crystal touched.

Alex agreed then shared, "It was your turn to lead us from the darkness."

T.R. looked puzzled.

Alex reminded him. "When we first met you thanked me for leading you from the darkness. A little hyperbole on your part I believe as you were only experiencing a nightmare."

"Alice." T. R.'s voice was melancholy. Distant.

Alex barely heard him say the name.

"Alice?" she questioned. "I thought we agreed on Alex. If we're changing our arrangement…"

T.R. could no longer hold the memory at bay. His eyes welled and he excused himself as he dabbed them with a kerchief. Alex saw the pain and was suddenly weighted by what she had somehow caused.

She put her hand to his. "T.R…have I offended you?"

T.R. pulled all composure from deep within. "No…not at all. It's just you resemble her. You resemble Alice."

"T.R. again, I don't know what I did but I am deeply sorry…."

"The dream you saved me from was unfortunately one that happened and the reason I'm here," T.R. disclosed on soft tones. "I lost my young wife Alice shortly after she gave birth to our daughter. My mother passed that same day. Within hours actually."

Alex put hand to mouth and shook her head in pain.

"It was a day void of light. I could do nothing to save them from the darkness."

"Mr. Roosevelt, I am so … I did not know." She took T.R. in her arms unsure of what else to do but feeling somewhere in being a woman that it was proper.

T.R. accepted the gift then pulled away and said, "Let's move on. How is bear? I've never had it."

Jasper watched from the edge of the flames the embrace between Alex and the stranger and hatred expanded in his soul.

13

Sylvane and Ferris shared a bottle of whiskey as they rode into the hills rationalizing that if their fellow hands back at the ranch were indulging then by God they would as well. As they rode they spoke of what a fine shot the new owner was, their love of mud packed bear paws, and how Bill's daughter had blossomed into a fine looking woman during her absence. From this the conversation turned to Jasper's delusion at even having a chance at Miss Alex and how riled he had been since T.R. arrived. Sylvane offered that Jasper would be better off visiting the brothel in Medora than wasting his time at courtship that would never happen.

By late afternoon they had reached the hills and were riding a trail through hardwoods feeling the whiskey's effect and having a good time. A dole of turkeys numbering seventeen crossed before them in a single file line of quick succession as they fled into the lower valley. Sylvane bid Ferris hold the whiskey bottle and raised his twelve gauge double barrel and took a fat hen with an offhanded shot. Sylvane gutted his bird and hung it from his saddle and told Ferris, "I kilt it. You'll be cooking it."

They made camp on a small rise overlooking the river just before sundown. Sylvane built up a cook fire while Ferris plucked the turkey and prepared it for the fire. They gorged on turkey and river mussels and ran through the bottle with joyful eagerness. They watched the sky blacken and then shine with thousands of stars and a half moon that illuminated the surroundings in a glow that Ferris said must be what heaven is like. This lighting was most prominent on the banks of the river. The white stone and sand of the riverbanks absorbed the angelic incandescence and reflected it many fold over. So too did the water reflect this light and in its flow and ebb over the rocks it was a hypnotic melody to those that listened. The two were feeling good, stuffed with meat, satisfied and carrying a good buzz.

"I can see why Jasper's been all over Miss Alex," Ferris confessed. "She is about ripe for the picking."

"We've watched her grow up!" Sylvane retorted.

"So?" Ferris came back.

"So nothing," Sylvane laughed. "I'd still pick that fruit. God almighty would I ever!"

The men chuckled and drank and admired the sky and drank some more. Such peace was it that Ferris was taken by Sylvane's sudden standing.

"What'cha doing?" Ferris asked.

"Taking a piss. Didn't know I had to check with you first."

"Well you do," Ferris laughed. "Go on and ask."

"Balls to you," Sylvane said as he walked from the fire ring in the direction of the river. "I' God is that?"

"Been that long since you seen your dick?" Ferris laughed. "You don't recognize it?"

"No. At the river down there. What the hell is that?"

Ferris stood and joined Sylvane at his side. The two watched a black form of four legs in the shallows of the water.

"Is that a bear?" Sylvane asked.

"Don't know what else it could be," Ferris admitted.

Sylvane returned to the fire ring and took his shotgun from the scabbard next to his saddle and returned to Ferris.

"Let's go," Sylvane whispered. "Down that way yonder to the left."

The men ambled through the scrub toward the figure in the water, their focus blurred by almost a bottle of whiskey shared between them. Inebriated as he was, Sylvane failed to recall that the gun he was carrying load meant for small game like turkey or rabbit.

And that only one barrel still held shot.

It was an error that would be his undoing.

14

T.R. and Bill were taking cigars on the porch following their evening meal. Rain clouds had built in the north and brought with them cooler temperatures. Lightning flashed in the distance and thunder rolled down the hills and across the prairies.

"Hard to believe," T.R. looked at the stogie in his hand. "But doctors prescribed me cigars when I was young as a way to battle my asthma."

"Can't say that that makes any sense to me," Bill replied. "Did it work?"

"No. Only hard work and exercise made a difference."

"Well, you certainly got plenty of that today," Bill reminded. "Shodding horses ain't light duty.

T.R. nodded, and then added, "Bauman's an interesting fellow. Strength of a bear despite his leg."

"Bauman's been here longer than I have. The way we argue, the hands secretly believe us to be an old married couple."

A flash of lightning illuminated a horse trotting toward the ranch. It appeared to carry no rider but as it came closer T.R. and Bill saw that a man lay slouched over the horse's neck. Jasper had seen the animal

from his chair outside the bunkhouse and ran out to meet it as it came

into the yard. T.R. and Bill and what ranch hands were about rushed to

meet it as well.

Ferris was beyond recognition and hovering somewhere just

above death. His face was streaked in blood, his nose half gone, and a

pulpy residue pooled in the socket where his left eye had once been. His

right hand carried only one finger and a partial thumb and his pants were

stiff with blood and his own waste. Jasper and the other hands pulled

him from the blood slicked horse and lay him on the ground. Alex

shrieked from the porch and Bill yelled for her to return inside and stay

there. Bauman ambled over and made the sign of the cross and ripped

the shirt from his body and tossed it to Jasper who placed it under the

head of the form that was once a man. Bill wrapped Ferris's lack of a

hand in a kerchief and commanded that someone get some water.

Bauman pressed his flask to Bill and Bill helped Ferris to sip.

"What happened?" Bill asked him in a voice so soft that all

around him knew he feared the reply.

Blood and saliva bubbled at Ferris's mouth as he tried to speak

and Bill wiped this from his face.

66

"Sylvane. Dead." He gasped. "Threw him through the air like a doll."

"What did?" Bill asked. "What was it?"

"Shot it in the face. Think it lost an eye."

Two Nights appeared from nowhere and listened intently.

"What lost an eye?" Bill begged. "What was it?"

Lightning flashed. Thunder boomed overhead. Errant raindrops fell.

"He had me down before I knew…"

Ferris's body collapsed on his last breath and his eye glazed over in relief. Jasper shook the body until Bill stopped him and took the crumpled shirt from under Ferris's head and draped it over the dead man's face. The men stood and in the silence they listened to T.R. who said, "O God, whose mercies cannot be numbered. Accept our prayers on behalf of thy servant and grant him an entrance into the land of light and joy, in the fellowship of thy saints; through Jesus Christ thy Son our Lord, who liveth and reigneth with thee and the Holy Spirit, one God, now and for ever. Amen."

All stood shocked for some time until Bill spoke, " Two Nights. Another grizzly? Could a bear have done…"

"It wasn't a bear and he knows what it was," Bauman announced. "It was God damned hell on Earth as it appeared to me four years ago. And this very night, he's back."

The men scoffed in half silence and looked to one another. Bill began to say something but couldn't before Bauman spoke again.

"Spring of '80 and that same beast killed two of my friends. Dragged one of our women to who knows where and turned me old overnight. It wasn't a grizzly but covered just the same. It was the shape of a man with the maw of a monster and eight foot tall at least."

"Is that what it was, what you found tracks of?" T.R. asked of Two Nights.

The men turned to the Indian and listened for explanation.

"It was Sésquac."

Jasper broke from the group to confront Two Nights.

"You knew there was some monster out there and instead a' killing it you took this Nancy Boy on a bear hunt?"

Bill came forward. "Jasper, that's enough."

Jasper turned from Two Nights and rushed at T.R.

"This man is dead because of you!"

"Jasper!" Bill shouted.

Jasper raged and dropped T.R. with a strong right and yelled, "Get up!"

Some of the men took Jasper from behind but T.R. waved them off as he stood.

"I don't want to fight you," he said as he removed his spectacles and put them in his pocket.

"Coward!" Jasper spat.

"I'm no coward," T.R. promised. "But I am afraid I'll hurt you."

Jasper cackled.

"I was runner-up in the Harvard Boxing Championship," T.R. continued.

"I've had enough!"

Jasper rushed forward and threw another right. T.R. ducked it with ease and countered with a right hook to the body, then a left-handed jab that sent Jasper stumbling backward.

"That's enough, Jasper!" T.R. commanded. "Stay down. There's no shame."

Jasper ran forward in a repeat of his earlier mistake. He threw a right then left neither of which connected. T.R. popped two quick jabs at Jasper's chin and dropped the aggressor to the ground.

The ranch hands called to Jasper, some telling him to stay down and others for him to rise.

Jasper stood and swung wild. T.R. stood back then went to work on Jasper's body in a succession of three body blows that sent Jasper to all fours and fighting for breath. When he came up again it was with a snap blade knife in his hand. He exploded forward in anger and T.R. dropped him once more to the ground. Jasper worked his mouth with his tongue and spat out a tooth in a wad of bloody phlegm. Bill came behind and took the knife from his hand and motioned for the ranch hands to pick him up. T.R. came forward with his hand outstretched to shake but Jasper would have none of it. He spat blood at T.R. and fought free from the men who held him and announced, "I'm riding out after this thing. Any of you cowards want to go you're welcome to it."

Bill corrected, "We ride out at first dawn. All of us."

The heavens opened and rain fell in sheets. Lightning flashed and thunder boomed.

"Jasper," Bill instructed, "Move Ferris in the barn and have Bauman look at your jaw."

15

Two Nights stood over Ferris's body which lay covered on a board set on sawhorses in the barn. All the men had left except Bauman and he and Two Nights stood in silence under the heavy rain that fell on the roof. Two Nights ran his hands above the body and uttered words in the tongue of his ancestors.

"That a prayer?" Bauman asked.

"More or less," Two Nights said. "Telling those who have gone before him that he is coming."

"Thought you were raised Christian," Bauman exclaimed.

"I was," Two Nights offered before walking to his horse stabled in a far stall.

Bauman followed on his crutch and said, "What is this thing, Sésquac?"

"It is what you saw."

"I'd say it was a monster."

"Some would say you were right. Legend says it's a wild man. Or the first man. Some say an ancient god."

"And you'd say?"

"I'd say that it was a monster and that it needs to be killed."

"And you're aiming to do that all by yourself tonight," Bauman figured.

Two Nights saddled his horse and placed his rifle in the scabbard.

"Ferris is dead because of me."

"That don't mean you should go off to get killed…"

"It is my responsibility…"

"Then maybe it's mine because I didn't do anything four years back and just cause your people have a name for it don't mean it makes it yours to deal with."

"That is true," Two Nights said. "But I will do what I can."

"Never took you for a fool," Bauman said.

"Then don't now."

Two Nights put heels to flank and rode out of the barn and into the rain. He passed the bunkhouse as a flash of lightning cracked across the sky and was off the property shortly after the echo of the following clap of thunder. He rode further into the storm and toward the hills that stood guard of the ranch below. His horse fought the slick mud and heavy streams of water that poured down the hill. Each bolt of lightening shook the horse and Two Nights did what he could to keep the animal calm and moving forward.

Rider and mount crossed the first hill and trailed the one above it and rode close to a stand of juniper that lay flattened by lightning only an hour earlier. The smell of electricity and burnt earth filled Two Nights' nostrils. His horse rattled hard and fought the reins and Two Nights snapped the reins and kicked the horse forward. The horse sidestepped and bucked and Two Nights heeled it hard once more.

And then Two Nights saw it.

Saw that it wasn't the remnants of a lightning strike that so spooked his horse. Rather, it was the scent of an apex predator.

It stood in a knot of dead cedar so twisted and gnarled that it resembled the skeleton of some animal from ancient times. Lighting spider webbed across the sky and in that flash Two Nights saw a beast who had been feared by man since his time began. It was over eight feet of carved muscle with a chest twice that of a man and arms of rolled iron. It roared with challenge, the force of its cry louder than the storm and more frightening than even the most fevered dream. Two Nights pulled the reins tight and reached for the gun in the scabbard. The gun was halfway to his shoulder when the darkness charged forward in a blur of violence and challenge. The gun was to his shoulder when the animal came up under the horse's neck and pushed the mount upward and over. Two Nights instinctively held tight to the reins and clamped his legs in a vise and he watched in slow motion as the world rolled over him. He heard the report of the rifle, the breaking of limbs, and the snap of his spinal column in two if not three places.

16.

The rain had stopped and the inside of the barn smelled of hay, horse, dampness and cigar smoke. Heavy drops still fell from the roof in front of the open doors and the area surrounding was slick with mud and the sky above covered in a black shroud. Bauman had almost finished construction of Ferris's coffin and all that remained was to nail the lid in place. The horses had listened to his hammering and to the sounds of the storm for more than an hour with little response until now. The twenty-one stabled horses cried and screeched and their eyes wide with sclera and their tails tucked. They rattled in their stalls and some kicked boards and others bit whatever was before them.

"I God if y'all ain't to making a racket," Bauman retched as he drove home another nail. He took a square head from his lips and held it against the lid and struck. The nail pinged sideways and to the barn floor. Bauman exhaled frustration and tossed the hammer on the lid and pulled the flask from the front pocket of his bib and drank. He was lowering his head from his pull on the whiskey when his eyes caught the hulking figure in the doorway.

The creature swayed slightly from side to side as it processed the smells of the barn. It grunted and dropped to all fours and ambled forward then stood and grunted again. Its right eye was seeping blood and pus and the face beneath it scabbed and matted with debris from what Bauman assumed was cartilage or bone shattered by Sylvane's twelve gauge. Bauman eased the hammer toward him and the sound of metal against rough wood caught the animal's attention and it turned to stare at the man with its one good eye. It bit at the air in a low bark and puffed its chest larger and growled like a dog cornered. Bauman hobbled back and then saw that his crutch was at the other end of the coffin. He stepped back once more and the beast matched his movements forward. Bauman thought of the rifle near his bunk and his instincts told him it was his only chance. He took one more step back and turned and made for the room behind him. The Cyclops vaulted forward and over the coffin and into Bauman's back. The old man crashed forward and his face went through the lit lantern hanging on the doorjamb. Glass shards pierced his cheek and neck and eye and the kerosene and the flame engulfed him. The creature jumped back and watched as Bauman flailed about and dropped to the floor. The fire spread through the barn like lightning and the horses exploded in screams. The barn was a cacophony of animal cries, devouring flames, and Bauman's last excursion of pain. The fire spread into Bauman's room and burned across his bed and to the lantern next to it. It boiled then exploded adding higher flames and more fuel for the fire. The beast backed from the torrent and dropped to all fours and roared at the turmoil.

Jasper and two ranch hands rushed through the open doors and the beast turned and screamed. It raged forward and upended the coffin in a show of strength then came to rest atop the first man it came to. The beast screamed over the fallen ranch hand and concaved his chest with two blows from anvil fists. Jasper turned and ran to the bunkhouse weaving and busting through the men running towards the fiery melee. The creature stood and roared at the thrall of oncoming men and vaulted forward and into them. Men screamed and scrambled to escape. Some fell in the mud and others stumbled on top of those that had fallen. The beast rushed through the men and pulled one from the muck by his leg and swung him into another and the sound of skull against skull cracked the air. The barn was totally engulfed in flames and the air was thick with smoke, singed hair and burning horseflesh. One horse broke from the burning barn like the legend Helios across the sky, its rear flanks ablaze. It slid in the mud and into the cook who had come running with lantern in hand. The collision of man and horse and lantern exploded in further flames and the cook stumbled forward and into the doorway of the bunkhouse. Two hands grabbed blankets from the beds nearest the entrance and did what they could to extinguish the burning man but this action only fanned the flames and set that building too to burning. Jasper came through the flames of the door with rifle in hand and aimed at the source of all their terror. He hesitated at the shot then lowered the rifle and shot instead the broken man below the predator whose arms were being ripped from its body. Jasper levered another shot and fired but hit only the mud below the beast.

The predator roared and burst forward and away from the chaos and onto the porch of the main house just as Bill and T.R. exited the building. The beast skidded into the outer wall on muddy feet and wet wood and raised itself immediately and grabbed the first threat it could. Bill's head was dwarfed by the huge hand and the back of his skull opened like a melon as the beast slammed it against the jamb of the open door. Blood and brain matter splattered across Alex's face as she rushed towards the door. She screamed at the violence and brutality of her father's killing and made to faint. The beast dropped Bill in a heap and reached for Alex as she fell. T.R. lunged and brought down the full force of the Bowie in his hand driving it into the monster's back shoulder. T.R. reached his arm around the juggernaut's neck for purchase and pulled the knife free but was thrown from the animal on the downward stroke of his knife. The beast howled in pain and grabbed Alex from her collapse and bulldozed into the darkness. T.R. stood just as Jasper appeared and pulled the ranch hand's rifle down as it fired.

"You'll hit Alice!" he screamed.

Jasper pushed T.R. aside, levered another round into the chamber of his rifle on the upswing and fired in vain. He screamed for Alex but wasn't heard over the cries of broken men, the howls of animals, and the roar of fire consuming two buildings.

17

Only five horses from the barn fire survived. Of those, two were so badly burned that they had to be put down and another most likely blind in one eye. The stock that was in the pasture at the time of the fire had scattered from the ranch immediate. Seven men were dead and another three so severely injured it would be months, if ever, they could return to their duties. The bunkhouse had burned to the ground and the barn reduced to a heap of smoldering coals, charred animals, and ash.

Jasper had chased after the animal firing into the darkness until his rifle went empty. When he returned to the scene he found T.R. and what few ranch hands were left dragging the bodies of the dead to a common area.

"Did you come across Two Nights?" T.R. asked.

Jasper stood in pallid shock.

"I need more..." Jasper searched for the words. "My bullets were in the bunk. Does Bill have any…"

"Jasper," T.R. stood in front of Jasper and held his eyes. "We'll get her back."

Jasper returned to the present. Anger boiled within him. "I know we will," he snapped. "Going after her now."

T.R. put his hand on Jasper's shoulder. He found the young man's eyes again and held them in his stare. "Did you see Two Nights?"

"What? No. I need them bullets."

"We need Two Nights to track..."

"Anybody could track that thing with the ground soaked like it is ..."

"Not once it gets into the hills."

"Well, I don't aim to let it get that far."

"It's dark. There are men here who need our help and we are not outfitted. We'll leave before dawn. You have my word. But we have to help those that we can now."

Jasper didn't like the idea but as the adrenalin subsided he saw that T. R. was right.

He hoped that he was also right about getting Alex back.

18

There was no tack or saddles to speak of so Jasper fashioned bridles from rope he found in the main house. He and T.R. each rode bareback with a rifle across their lap and pistols on their belts. The going was slow in the pre-dawn darkness given the mud and the skittishness of the mounts. They found the first signs of the animal's stress at the base of the first hill. The wallow told that the beast had rolled in the mud and a smaller impression showed that Alex had been there as well. Jasper dismounted and studied the area further. He traced the area where Alex had lain and said, "She didn't move once placed here. Guess she's unconscious."

T.R. theorized she had hit her head on the door when taken or suffered a jar while being carried or simply succumbed to stress.

Jasper gestured to a small pool of blood and detailed, "He rolled here to close his wound. Animals will do that. How well did you stick him?"

T.R. pulled the Bowie from his belt, held it aloft and said, "To the hilt."

"Then he's hurt bad," Jasper said as he mounted his horse.

The men rode up the hill and despite the change in terrain were able to track the animal to the summit of the first rise. They rode through heavy juniper and needled scrub and there found the occasional streaks of mud and blood that told them they were on the right trail. By mid-morning though their luck had vanished. They could find no tracks or sign of the beast or of Alex. Jasper grew angry at the loss of their way. Angry at himself and angry at his train of thought. Why did it take her? What would it do to her? Was there still time to save her?

His thoughts were interrupted by T.R.'s exclamation of, "Buzzards."

Jasper looked at the mass of black circling to the east and the two headed toward it. They passed a juniper shattered by lightning and not far past it Jasper found horse tracks. They followed them to a story of troughed mud and earth that pushed over a sharp drop. T.R. and Jasper dismounted simultaneously and made their way to the edge.

"My God," T.R. exclaimed.

"Sweet Mother of God," Jasper echoed.

Twenty feet below on a shelf of jutted stone barely large enough to accommodate it was a knot of horse and man, bone and flesh. Only

Two Night's head was visible, his body hidden beneath an animal so broke and cut it barely resembled a horse at all.

"Two Nights!" T.R. yelled hoping against hope for an answer. "Two Nights!"

Two Night's eyes opened and he gasped the word, "Here."

"I'm coming down," T.R. promised.

"You can't..." Jasper had barely gotten the words out before T.R. was pulling the halter from his horse. He undid the makeshift lead of rope and tied it to end of his bullwhip.

"Yours," T.R. gestured. "Come on now."

Jasper undid the tie of ropes and added it to T.R.'s piecemeal cordage.

"That ledge looks to be barely holding on," Jasper pleaded. "And it's at least another twenty feet drop down below that."

"Yes, and if I fall I'll die in the trees below trying to save a good man."

Jasper nodded in understanding and tied one end of the rope to a stump near the ledge and ran the slack of the rope around the strength of his back. T.R. took the handle of the bullwhip and looked over the edge. He looked to Jasper who tightened his grip and flexed his back and nodded that he was ready. T.R. stepped back over the ledge and Jasper lowered him to the shelf below.

T.R. called the feet during his descent.

"Fifteen…Ten…Almost."

When he reached the shelf, he straddled the horse, and while still holding the whip, leaned over Two Nights.

T.R. leaned over Two Nights and asked, "How bad?"

Two Nights answered with resigned eyes. T.R. assessed the melee he straddled and reached for the canteen hanging from the pommel of the broken horse. The strap ran under the horse and was caught on something so T.R. cut it with his Bowie and held the vessel to Two Night's lips so he could drink.

"I saw the smoke," Two Nights uttered in a voice that was cracked and forced.

"Bad; seven dead. Bill's one of them."

"I'll join them soon."

"Don't talk that way," T.R. insisted. "I'll have you out of here in no time."

"No," Two Nights declared. He closed his eyes as if deep in thought and opened them and looked at T.R. and said, "Don't make me ask."

T.R. knew the question of which his newest friend referred. He searched his emotions and looked over the ledge to see if there was anything else that could be done. He ran his hand over the Indian's head and Two Nights relished in the last physical touch of a friend in the living. He closed his eyes and nodded slightly. T.R. pulled his Colt as quietly as he could and eased the hammer back with the loudest click that he had ever heard. He set the barrel to just before Two Night's closed eye and fired.

The pistol shot echoed down over the canyon and up over the highland. Jasper fought the rope to the edge of the cliff and looked down at T.R. He saw a small black hole where Two Night's eye had been and the splatter of blood and brain matter beneath his head. Jasper was arrested at the sight but a roar shot from the cedars behind him turned him. The beast raged forward on four legs in a sideways gait. Jasper yelled "Hold on," and dropped the rope. He drew his Colt .44 and took aim. The sound of Alex screaming from somewhere behind the creature caused a blink in Jasper's actions. He fired and dirt exploded just past the beast. He fired again, this time the shot taking a tuft of skin off the creature's shoulder. Jasper stepped back and fired again as the rocks beneath him gave way and he fell. He somehow managed to grab the rope but his grip wasn't set and he shot down the strand with no control of his person. T.R. braced himself and grabbed Jasper by the waist as he passed and the two fell back against the face of the shelf.

T.R. looked up to see rocks and earth giving way and the monster tumbling over. He squeezed Jasper's hands tight to the rope and threw him with all his might. Jasper swung off of the shelf just as the beast landed onto the body of the horse. It righted itself onto unsure footing and screamed. T.R. pulled his Colt and the shelf gave way. Rock and debris, the beast and the horse, T.R. and Two Night's bodies crashed downward ripping through the tops of cedars to the ground below. T.R.'s world went sideways and he strained to see straight. The beast lay pinned beneath the horse, and T.R. stood vised between it and Two Night's body. T.R. pulled his leg from under the horse and backed away on hands and knees over to Two Nights and onto a jumble of stone and broken limbs. Jasper yelled for T.R. from above and his cry was echoed by Alex's cry somewhere above him. T.R. saw that his left leg was bent at the knee and he knew the break was bad. He yelled up to Jasper, "Get to Alex! Climb!"

The beast pant-grunted and lifted the shattered horse off of it. It screamed as its leg collapsed and T.R. watched as its femur shot past his kneecap and out of its lower thigh. T.R. realized the pistol was no longer in his hand and he pulled its sister from his belt. He drew a bead on the center of the great beast's chest and fired. The hammer fell with a dim click. T.R. thumbed the hammer back once more and saw that it was bent and all but useless. The beast dropped to all fours and dragged itself over the horse and towards T.R. The animal's roar was deafening at such close quarters and the stench of rot and blood from its howl scoured T.R.'s nostrils. T.R. pulled his Bowie and crept backward on the uneven terrain. The beast lunged and shattered the limb beneath T.R.'s head with a slam of its fist. The beast pulled back and came down with all its might. T.R. careened his head from the creature's blow and plunged the Bowie halfway into the neck of the animal. Blood shot from its jugular and the ape howled in pain. It pulled the knife from its neck and a torrent of blood shot sideways in arterial spray. T.R. rolled to his belly and crawled beneath the flailing giant to Two Night's body. He pulled the Indian's pistol and rolled over and fired into the ape's back. The ape turned to his pain and T.R. fanned the gun. The air boomed with gunshots and the sounds of bullets slamming into flesh and the death throes of an animal that is the last of its kind. Sésquac dropped to its knees and fell forward in death and onto T.R. and as it had when the grizzly fell on him, T.R. felt the breath being crushed out of him and his world went dark.

The black suit was the first piece of formal attire Jasper had ever worn and he pulled at his collar and rolled his shoulders in discomfort. Alex slapped his hand and reminded him that the event was a solemn one and not to fuss. Jasper frowned and nodded with the look of a boy who had just been scolded. He looked over the sea of suited men and women in their Sunday finest, amazed at the number of people present. He knew that T.R. was well known but the sheer size of the crowd was beyond his vocabulary. He turned to Alex and watched as she dabbed tears from her eyes. Jasper reached for her hand and took it in his. She faced him and smiled then suddenly exploded, "My word! Is that Geronimo?"

Jasper turned to see the figure in question. "Sure as hell looks like it. Guess everybody turned out to see this."

"But Geronimo?" Alex asked in disbelief.

T.R. walked to the podium set upon the East Portico of the Capital and declared, "My fellow-citizens, no people on earth have more cause to be thankful than ours, and this is said reverently, in no spirit of boastfulness in our own strength, but with gratitude to the Giver of Good who has blessed us with the conditions which have enabled us to achieve so large a measure of well-being and of happiness."

T.R.'s inaugural address continued on that Sunday March 4, 1905 and in that speech he assured the world, "I have fought monsters of every kind and as your president I shall continue to do so and on that you have my word."

The crowd cheered.

T.R. shall return!

About the Author

Gayne C. Young is the best selling author of *And Monkeys Threw Crap At Me: Adventures In Hunting, Fishing, And Writing*, the Editor of *Game Trails Online*, the official online magazine of the Dallas Safari Club, and a columnist for and feature contributor to *Outdoor Life* and *Sporting Classics* magazines. His work has appeared in magazines such as *Shooting Sportsman, Petersen's Hunting, Texas Sporting Journal, Sports Afield, Gray's Sporting Journal, Under Wild Skies, Hunter's Horn, Spearfishing*, and many others. His screenplay, *Eaters Of Men* was optioned in 2010 by the Academy Award winning production company of Kopelson Entertainment. In January 2011, Gayne C. Young became the first American outdoor writer to interview Russian Prime Minister, and former Russian President, Vladimir Putin.

Again, I greatly appreciate you taking the time to read my work.

Please consider leaving a review wherever you bought the book or telling your friends about my book to help spread the word.

Please visit me at my website www.gaynecyoung.com.

Made in the USA
Lexington, KY
25 November 2014